ALICIA HAS A BAD DAY

LISA JAHN-CLOUGH

Houghton Mifflin Co. Boston

For Jack Gantos and for my grandfather

Library of Congress Cataloging-in-Publication Data
Jahn-Clough, Lisa.
    Alicia has a bad day / Lisa Jahn-Clough.
        p. cm.
    Summary: When Alicia can't seem to cheer up,
she tries going back to bed.
    RNF ISBN 0-395-69454-X   PA ISBN 0-618-26011-0
    [1. Mood (Psychology) — Fiction.] I. Title.
PZ7.J153536Al 1994   94-4520
[E] — dc20   CIP
                                                    AC

Printed in Mexico
RRD 10 9 8 7 6 5 4 3

Hello! My name is Alicia.
This is my dog, Neptune.
I am generally a very happy person.

But not always.
Some days I am miserable.

Today I am so miserable I don't want
to get out of bed. Neptune doesn't
even lick my face like he usually does.

Eventually I do get up.
But all I can do is sit and mope.

After I mope I lie on the floor and stare at the ceiling. The cracks make faces at me.

Then I play music very loud
and I dance very fast.

I stand on my head. I listen to my heart beat.
But I am still miserable.

Finally, I grab my notebook
and my red crayon and go outside.

I walk into the woods,
stepping on ant hills as I go. HA!

I sit down on a stump. I write the word
LUGUBRIOUS in my notebook.

Lugubrious is my favorite miserable word.
It means dark and dreary.

It is dark and dreary in my heart.

A big, gray cloud covers the sun.
It starts to rain and ants crawl up my cheek!

On my way home I trip.
I land in a gooey mud puddle! Grrrr.

I run upstairs. I shout as loud as I can,
"I AM MISERABLE!"

I crawl to the darkest, dreariest place I know.

Under my bed.

I feel something soft and warm.
It's Neptune! He licks my face.

We go outside to play, and
the world is a little less lugubrious.